Bartimouse

& the Harvest Garden

Words by Christina Goodings
Pictures by Maxwell Lawrence Dorsey

LION
Children's Books

It was a bright day in early summer. The sky was blue and the sun was shining; but Bartimouse and Emma were a bit worried.

Bartimouse

Emma

In the afternoon, when the children came for stories and games in the little hall, Debbie marched them all out to her patch of ground.

'Today,' she announced grandly, 'we are going to
sow seeds and grow our very own vegetables.'

They all set to work.

Some marked long grooves in the soil and others sprinkled seeds in them.

Others covered the grooves and watered the rows.

Debbie labelled everything.

When they all went back inside the hall, Bartimouse and Emma stayed to look at the new garden.

Every day the children came to look at the garden.

Sometimes it was sunny.

Sometimes it was rainy.

One day, Debbie saw Bartimouse's plant.

'Who planted that, I wonder?' she
said. 'I decided not to plant any runner
bean seeds.'

The next day, she brought three very long sticks to mark Bartimouse's plant.

runner bean

As summer passed, the plants all grew. Some had great green leaves. Others had bright bulging roots. Yet others had fruits that grew larger every day.

Bartimouse's plant grew very tall. It wrapped itself round the sticks. Bright flowers appeared. When the petals fell, the children saw tiny green pods growing where the flowers had been.

At last, Debbie said it was time to harvest the garden. Everyone began to pick and soon the garden looked quite empty.

'Stop now,' said Debbie. 'We have enough for us. Let's leave the rest for the little creatures that live all around. They need a harvest too.'

Under a harvest moon, Bartimouse and
Emma gathered all they needed for a feast.

The next morning, while Emma wrote the invitations, Bartimouse began washing the vegetables.

While Bartimouse took the invitations round to their friends, Emma chopped the vegetables ready to make a pot of soup.

Up in the little hall, Debbie and
the children were just as busy.

Not everyone was working quite
as hard as Emma.

And over in the fields, mice were reading their invitations.

In the afternoon, everyone came
with gifts to share a harvest meal.

Debbie stayed late, clearing up at the end.
She came to take one last look at the garden.

'Still a few bean pods,' she said
aloud as she looked
at Bartimouse's
plant. 'I'll leave
those to ripen,
so we can all
plant runner
beans next
year.'